S0-BZZ-072

Now and Forever
May You always be able
To Touch the Hand of
GOD"
Gene
Eugene J Phelan

TO TOUCH
THE HAND
OF GOD

To Mary Loretta Phelan

Now and Forever,

May you always be able to "Touch the Hand of God"

Copyright © 2016 by Eugene J. Phelan

MCP Books
322 1st Ave North, 5th Floor
Minneapolis, MN 55401
612.455.2293
www.mcpbooks.com

All rights reserved. No part of this publication may be reproduced, stored in a retrieval system, or transmitted, in any form or by any means, electronic, mechanical, photocopying, recording, or otherwise, without the prior written permission of the author.

ISBN-13: 978-1-63413-952-6
LCCN: 2016900285

Distributed by Itasca Books

Cover Design by Penny Weber
Typeset by T. Schaeppi

Printed in the United States of America

TO TOUCH THE HAND OF GOD

Eugene J. Phelan

Illustrations by Penny Weber

MCP BOOKS
MINNEAPOLIS, MN

On a Saturday morning, the sun slowly rose and brightened the early morning sky. Walter sat on the living room couch, sipping coffee, reading the morning paper off and on, and listening to the news in the background from the television. Karen, his daughter, just seven years old, was lying on her tummy on the rug in front of him and reading her storybook.

Walter glanced up from his newspaper and looked at all the pictures on the walls and in frames on the entertainment center. His heart still ached, and he was terribly depressed. Sometimes it took all of his strength just to get moving for breakfast, work, cooking, cleaning, laundry, and yard work, and then the long hours at night, alone, staring at the ceiling, hoping for sleep.

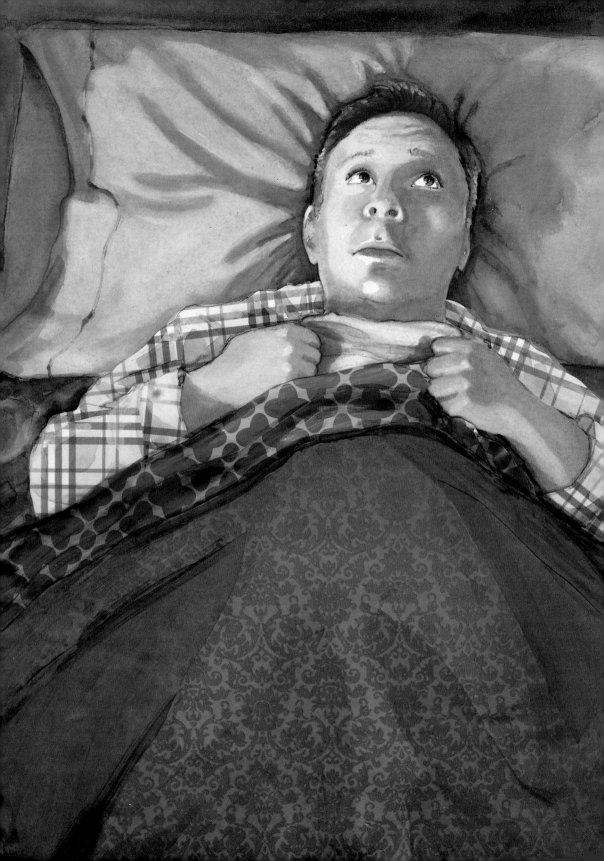

He wasn't good at hiding his feelings, and even if he was, children have a powerful radar to sense things, especially with family.

"Dad, you miss Mom a lot, don't you?"

"Yes, hon. I do. But don't worry. Everything will turn out all right."

A religious Christian man, he knew this was true, but the depression and pain still cut deep into his soul. He forced himself to focus on all the wonderful gifts he enjoyed as a parent.

Just recently he taught Karen to ride a two-wheel bicycle. The joy of victory and accomplishment on her face was incredible. It only happens once, and then it is gone forever. But the day remained a treasured memory.

And re-living your own childhood memories through your children? A gift that keeps giving for a lifetime. Karen learning to swim, and then diving down to grab shells and stones, bursting out of the water, racing her father to shore, and Walter letting her win by just a hand or two. Her first time being tall enough for a roller coaster, their hands in the air as they yelled. Her first time in a school play.

I am blessed, he thought. How could anyone want to miss these precious moments? Karen brought him back to the present.

"Dad, what are we going to do today?"

The breakfast dishes were clean, but there was yard work to do, the lawn to be mowed, and the week's laundry to be done.

"Karen, I have to mow the lawn after the morning dew dries up. Maybe we can go somewhere after lunch."

"Okay, Dad."

What he wanted was to crawl back into bed and sleep for a week or two.

"Dad, can I ask you a question?"

Walter always turned these requests into a silly joke.

"No, Karen."

"Well, what happens . . ."

Laughing, Walter interrupted. "Hey, I said no!"

"*Daaaaaad!*" she said, stretching out the word and laughing.

"What is it, Pumpkin?"

"What happens when you hold up a mirror to another mirror?"

Suddenly, Walter was six years old again, and asking the same question, a small child holding up a mirror and seeing the magical result.

"Karen, let's find out."

Digging through the closet, he lifted up the toolbox. He thought about the full-size mirror on a frame in the bedroom. A hand mirror was not good enough. Not this time. No.

"Karen, we need to use the cordless drill."

In the other bedroom, there was another full-length mirror attached to the back of the door. With the drill, Walter unscrewed the four corner screws with Karen assisting him. She collected the screws in a paper cup, and on the last screw, she used the drill while Walter held on to the mirror.

"What happens now, Dad?"

Smiling, he said, "We are going to find out right now."

Walter carried the mirror under his arm to the bedroom, with Karen close behind.

"Karen, stand in front of the mirror and I'll hold the other one behind you."

Walter held up the mirror behind Karen and watched her reflection multiply into infinity. He tilted the mirror a few degrees in different directions so that Karen got the full effect.

With her eyes growing and glowing in amazement, she yelled,

"DADDY, LOOK AT ALL OF THE ME'S!"

She glanced back and forth from the mirror behind her to the large framed one in front.

"Daddy, in your mirror, how far back does it go?"

"It keeps reflecting and goes back forever, Karen."

"Wow! You mean it has NO beginning?"

"That's right. No beginning."

Karen put her hand on the mirror and touched the hand of her reflection. She turned to the framed mirror and did the same, her hands extended and touching both.

"How far does this one go, Dad? The same?"

"Yes, Karen. It just keeps reflecting and has no end."

Karen kept glancing back and forth at all the other Karens hand in hand in hand, on and on.

"Dad. No beginning and no end? You mean like God?"

"Yes, honey. No beginning and no end."

Karen started screaming in joy and happiness. "DADDY, I'M TOUCHING THE HANDS OF GOD!"

Watching his daughter's happiness healed Walter's heart in a way it never had before, and may never happen again in the same way. He leaned the mirror against the bed and they both stood between the mirrors and eternity. They took out Walter's cell phone and took picture after picture from every angle imaginable. Laughing at all the Walters and Karens laughing into forever, finally, they were all laughed out and sat on the rug giggling.

"Daddy, that was fun!"

"I can think of something else that's fun. The yard and the laundry can wait until after dinner. Today is a perfect day for sand castles and swimming at the beach. You load up the car, and I'll get the cooler and make sandwiches and snacks."

"All right, Dad. That sounds great!"

With a lighter step and a lighter heart, Walter walked out the back door to the garage to get the cooler. Karen was in her room getting changed into her swimsuit and would soon gather pails, plastic shovels, an umbrella, blanket, towels, and anything else needed. She was the house expert on loading the car for a beach trip.

Standing in the garage, Walter said a silent prayer.

"Thank you, God, for the miracle of this day. Thank you for holding my daughter's hand . . . and mine."

THE END.